Winter Magic

127

For Marcus

Scholastic Children's Books
Commonwealth House, 1-19 New Oxford Street
London WC1A 1NU, UK
a division of Scholastic Ltd
London ~ New York ~ Toronto ~ Sydney ~ Auckland
Mexico City ~ New Delhi ~ Hong Kong

First published in hardback in the UK by Scholastic Ltd, 2004
This paperback edition first published in the UK by Scholastic Ltd, 2005

Copyright © Julie Monks, 2004

ISBN 0 439 97373 2

All rights reserved

Printed in Singapore

2 4 6 8 10 9 7 5 3 1

The right of Julie Monks to be identified as the author and illustrator
of this work has been asserted by her in accordance with
the Copyright, Designs and Patents Act, 1988.

Winter Magic

Julie Monks

Hippo

Out of the window
all is white.

Snow covers the hills
and everything looks
magical.

We put on
woollen hats and
Wellington boots.

Outside, the
snow goes
crunch,
crunch,
crunch
under our feet.

We try to catch
snow flakes,
but they disappear
in our hands.

We help make a snowman.
Our footprints leave
patterns all around him.

The snow dances and swirls in the sky. The light makes shadows on the white ground.

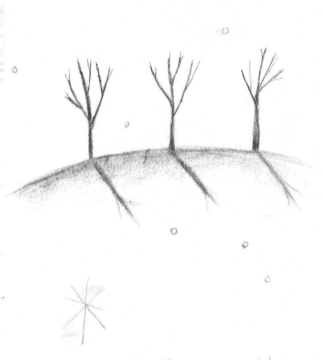

The snow makes winter magic.

Over the hill
dances a hare
dressed in white,
skippety skip.

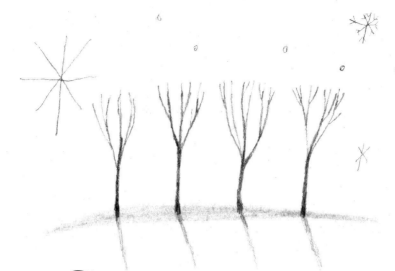

$\mathcal{T}$he shadows of the trees
become the antler of deer.

We hide underneath.

The snow-covered hill becomes the soft back of a white bear.

$\mathcal{W}$ho carries us on his back . . .
all the way home.

We whisper 'goodnight'
and the stars twinkle in the sky.